Molly's
Short Story
Collection

BELONGS TO

_____

_____

_____

DATE

Read all of the novels about Molly:

· MOLLY ·

The adventures of *Molly McIntire*
continue in this keepsake collection of
short stories. Molly's growing up in a world
of wartime changes. Life on the home front
means doing without things like new
clothes and toys. For Molly, it also means
doing without her dad, who is overseas
helping wounded soldiers. With resource-
fulness, Molly discovers that working
together doesn't just help the war effort. It
makes a big difference in her own life, too.

Discover more about Molly's world in
these heartwarming stories of hard work
and patriotism.

Molly's
SHORT STORY
COLLECTION

By VALERIE TRIPP

ILLUSTRATIONS BY NICK BACKES

VIGNETTES BY SUSAN MCALILEY, NICK BACKES,

PHILIP HOOD, AND KEITH SKEEN

★ American Girl™

Published by Pleasant Company Publications

Questions or comments? Call 1-800-845-0005,
visit our Web site at **americangirl.com**, or write to Customer Service,
American Girl, 8400 Fairway Place, Middleton, WI 53562-0497.

Printed in China
06 07 08 09 10 11 LEO 12 11 10 9 8 7 6 5 4 3 2

Cataloging-in-Publication Data
available from the Library of Congress.

PICTURE CREDITS

TABLE OF CONTENTS

MOLLY'S FAMILY
AND FRIENDS

MOLLY'S FAMILY

DAD
*Molly's father, a doctor
who is somewhere in
England, taking care of
wounded soldiers*

MOM
*Molly's mother, who
holds the family together
while Dad is away*

MOLLY
*A girl growing up
on the home front
in America during
World War Two*

JILL
*Molly's older sister,
who is always trying to
act grown-up*

RICKY
*Molly's older
brother—a big pest*

BRAD
*Molly's younger
brother—a little pest*

GRANPA
*Molly's grandfather, who
doesn't like change*

GRAMMY
*Molly's grandmother,
who always keeps the
cookie jar full*

AUNT ELEANOR
*Molly's aunt, who
wants to do her part
to win the war*

MOLLY'S FRIENDS

LINDA
*One of Molly's best friends,
a practical schemer*

SUSAN
*Molly's other best friend,
a cheerful dreamer*

MRS. GILFORD
*The housekeeper,
who rules the roost when
Mom is at work*

MISS CAMPBELL
*Molly's teacher, who keeps her
third graders on their toes*

MISS BUTTERNUT
*The counselor at
Camp Gowonagin*

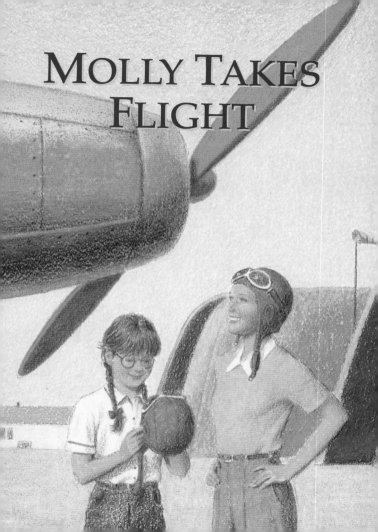

MOLLY TAKES FLIGHT

MOLLY TAKES
FLIGHT

Here it is!" cried Molly McIntire. "Here's the farm!" Molly stuck her head out the truck window as Granpa turned in at the gate.

"Hold on!" Granpa shouted over the truck's noisy engine. "The ruts in this drive are worse than ever. Your grandmother's after me to smooth them. But I figure the ruts keep trouble out."

Molly smiled as the truck bounced along. Granpa said the same thing about

the ruts every summer.

It was August, and Molly had come to visit her grandparents and her Aunt Eleanor on their farm. Every summer before this, Molly's whole family had made the trip together. But this summer, Molly was by herself.

Coming to the farm alone was only

one of many changes in Molly's life since the war began. First, Dad joined the army and went to England to take care of wounded soldiers. Then Mom started to work for the Red Cross. Molly's sister Jill was a volunteer at the Veterans' Hospital this summer. Molly's older brother Ricky was never home because he had a job mowing lawns, and her younger brother Brad was going to day camp.

Molly felt as if change had whooshed through her life and set everything spinning. So she was reassured to see, as the truck rattled past the fields and the barn and the swimming hole, that here at the farm everything looked the same. Granpa didn't grow crops anymore, but he still had chickens, an old horse, a few cows, and a big vegetable garden. Molly loved the way the farm seemed to have fallen asleep long ago. It was peaceful and unchanging.

Granpa stopped the truck in front of the farmhouse. Molly jumped out and ran straight into the kitchen and straight into Grammy's arms for a hug. "Hello, Grammy!" she said.

"Hello, dear girl," said Grammy. "We're glad you're here."

Molly took a deep breath. Dad always said that you could blindfold him and fly him around the world, but he'd know the instant he was back in Grammy's kitchen because of the smell.

It was a delicious combination of
strawberries, buttered toast, maple syrup,
and scrubbing powder. Molly wished
Dad were with her now in the familiar
kitchen. The sun shone through the
windows onto the white enamel table
and made patterns of light on the shiny
floor. When Molly was little, she thought
Grammy's cookie jar was magic
because it was never empty. It
was comforting to see it sitting
in its usual place on the shelf.

"Where's Aunt Eleanor?"
Molly asked.

"Oh, Eleanor's off and away," said
Grammy.

"As usual," muttered Granpa.

5

Grammy frowned and shook her head at him.

Molly was disappointed. What did Granpa mean? It was *not* usual for Aunt Eleanor to be gone. Every other year she had been there to welcome Molly to the farm.

Granpa pushed open the screen door and said, "Come on, Molly. Want to help me choose a melon for supper?"

"Yes, sir!" said Molly. She followed Granpa out into the warm summer evening.

By the time Molly and Granpa got back from the melon patch, Aunt Eleanor

was in the kitchen, setting the table
for supper. Aunt Eleanor was Molly's
mother's sister. She had short, curly hair
and wasn't much taller than Molly. Aunt
Eleanor moved in such a quick, light
manner that she reminded Molly of a
bird. Just now she swooped over, gave
Molly a hug, and asked as she always
did, "What's up, Doc?"

Molly replied as *she* always did,
"Not much, Dutch!"

"Wash up, girls," said Grammy.
"Supper's ready."

Molly was eating her second piece of
melon when she said, "Aunt Eleanor, I
bet I'll swing higher than you on the rope
swing at the swimming hole tomorrow."

Aunt Eleanor cleared her throat. "I'm afraid I can't swim with you tomorrow, Molly," she said.

Molly was surprised. "But we always go swimming on the first day of my visit," she protested. "We do the same thing every year."

"Eleanor, are you going to tell Molly that this year isn't going to be the same as every other year?" said Granpa. He sounded as if he was cross with Aunt Eleanor.

"Now, Frank!" said Grammy quickly. She looked at Molly and Aunt Eleanor. "Why don't you girls go outside and count shooting stars? Your chart is in the barn."

"Okay," said Molly. "Come on, Aunt Eleanor."

It was a tradition that Molly and Aunt Eleanor went outside to stargaze every night after supper and kept a count of all the shooting stars they spotted. Tonight they found the star chart and flopped down on a stack of hay. It was still warm from the sun, though the sky was dark now and crowded with stars.

Molly scanned the sky to be sure the North Star was just where it was supposed to be, at the end of a group of stars called the Little Dipper. She smiled when she saw it. The North Star had become very important to Molly. She turned to Aunt

9

Eleanor to tell her about it. "Before he left, Dad told me to look for the North Star every night," she said, "because—"

Aunt Eleanor interrupted. "You miss your dad a lot, don't you, Molly?" she asked. Her voice was very sad.

"I do," said Molly. "That's why—" But Aunt Eleanor sighed so deeply that

10

Molly stopped explaining to ask, "Aunt Eleanor, what's going on? Is Granpa mad at you?"

"Seems like it," said Aunt Eleanor.

"Why?" asked Molly.

"Well," said Aunt Eleanor, "I think because I've applied to join the WASPs— they're the Women's Airforce Service Pilots."

Molly sat up and looked at Aunt Eleanor. "You're going to be a pilot in the Air Force?" she exclaimed. "You're going to fly fighter planes and drop bombs and be in the war?"

"No," said Aunt Eleanor. "WASPs don't fly combat missions. They test planes, and train other pilots, and fly planes from one airfield to another. They help the Air Force do its job."

"But will you have to go away?" Molly wanted to know.

"Yes," said Aunt Eleanor. "If I'm accepted, I'll have to leave immediately."

Molly felt as if the earth beneath her were falling away. *This dumb old war,* she thought. *It's changing everything. First Dad left, and now Aunt Eleanor.*

"What do Grammy and Granpa say?" Molly asked.

Aunt Eleanor shook her head. "Nothing," she said. "Your granpa hates changes. He says he doesn't fix the ruts because they keep trouble out. But what he really means is that the ruts keep *change* out. He likes being cut off from the world. He wants to pretend there is no war. That's why he won't talk to me about flying." She was quiet for a minute. Then she asked, "What do *you* think, Molly?"

"I don't know," said Molly quickly. But that wasn't true. She knew exactly what she thought. She hated the idea of Aunt Eleanor going away. She hated it so much, it made her angry—angry at the war, angry at the world, and even a little bit angry at Aunt Eleanor.

Aunt Eleanor stood and dusted off her pants. "Come on," she said. "I guess all the stars are staying put tonight. Let's go in."

The next few days were long and hot and dull for Molly. Aunt Eleanor went off every morning before Molly was awake and didn't come home until supper time. Molly did all the things she usually loved doing on the farm. She collected eggs, visited the cows, picked vegetables for Grammy, climbed up to the hayloft, waded in the brook, swung on the rope swing over the swimming hole, and one day even helped Granpa make ice cream. But nothing was as much fun without Jill and Ricky and Brad—and especially without Aunt Eleanor.

One night, Aunt Eleanor still had not come home even when Molly went to bed. The night was so hot and sticky that Molly couldn't get to sleep. She stared out the open window for a while, looking at the North Star, thinking about Dad and hoping for a breeze, but the air was heavy and still. Nothing came through the window but the raspy noise of the crickets.

Molly kicked off the sheets and brushed her sweaty bangs off her forehead. *This summer's visit to the farm is no good,* Molly thought, *and it's all Aunt Eleanor's fault.*

Just then, Aunt Eleanor tiptoed into Molly's room. "Are you awake?" she whispered.

"Sort of," said Molly. She rolled onto

her side and punched her pillow to make it fluff up. "Where have you been?"

"At the airfield," said Aunt Eleanor. "I want to practice flying as many hours as I can."

Molly flopped onto her back. "It seems like you've practiced about a million hours since I've been here," she said. "By the way, I saw two shooting stars tonight. You missed them."

Aunt Eleanor sat down on Molly's bed. "Molly," she said. "I'm sorry—"

"No, you are not!" said Molly. "You don't care about Grammy or Granpa or me or the farm. All you care about is flying. You don't have to leave the farm and go away and be a WASP. You *want* to. You're going to leave just like Dad did, and I'll never see you, and I'll have to worry all the time that you're hurt or lost or—" Molly stopped.

Aunt Eleanor looked as if she might cry. She tried to hug Molly, but Molly jerked her shoulder away.

Aunt Eleanor didn't move. Then she whispered, "Good night, Molly," and left.

The next morning there were still a few stars shining when Aunt Eleanor shook Molly awake. "Get dressed," said Aunt Eleanor. "I have a surprise for you."

Molly dressed and stumbled down to the kitchen. Aunt Eleanor handed her a piece of toast and led her out the door to her car.

"Where are we going?" asked Molly.

"You'll see," said Aunt Eleanor.

Soon enough, Molly did see. They were going to the airfield. The big silver hangars looked eerie in the dim morning light, and the small planes parked in front of them looked as delicate as dragonflies.

Aunt Eleanor parked the car. Molly followed her across the pavement to one of the small planes. "This is the plane I fly," said Aunt Eleanor. "It's a PT-19." She patted the nose of the plane as if it were a horse she liked. Then she handed Molly a helmet. "Put it on," she said.

"We're going up."

"Me?" squeaked Molly.

Aunt Eleanor winked as she helped Molly climb into the plane. "Don't worry," she said. "You know I've practiced flying a lot. How much was it? I think you said about a million hours already."

Molly fastened her seat belt and

looked out the small windshield of the plane. The sky was brightening to blue now, and all the stars were gone. Aunt Eleanor spoke to a man over the radio. In a scratchy voice he gave her permission to take off.

The plane was noisier than Granpa's truck, and the runway seemed just as bumpy as the rutted drive into the farm. Molly gripped the edge of her seat as the little plane picked up speed. Faster, faster, faster it went until, smooth as a bird on a breeze, it lifted off the ground and climbed into the huge blue sky.

Molly smiled. She was flying! It was exhilarating—just like when she let go of the rope swing far out over the water and, for a moment or two, she was not on land or on the rope or in the water but zooming through the air. She understood now why Aunt Eleanor loved flying.

As they flew along, Molly looked out at the fields below. They looked green and tidy and well cared for. The blue river wound like a lazy snake past silver silos and red barns and farmhouses white as chalk.

"I never saw the world this way before," Molly shouted to Aunt Eleanor over the engine's roar. "I never realized how pretty it is."

Aunt Eleanor smiled. "Look at this," she said. She made the plane tilt to one

21

side and then swoop low. "Here's the place I love the best—our farm. It's the prettiest spot of all, isn't it?"

Molly looked down and saw Grammy and Granpa's house and barn, the vegetable garden and the melon patch, the swimming hole and the rutted drive. "Yup," she said, "it's the prettiest spot of all."

Aunt Eleanor steered the plane in a wide, slow curve and headed it back to the airfield. All too soon, the plane landed with a bump and then skidded to a stop in front of the hangar.

As Molly climbed out of the plane, Aunt Eleanor asked, "Did you like flying?"

"I *loved* it," said Molly.

"I knew you would," said Aunt Eleanor happily. "Come on. I'd better drive you home."

In the car Molly said, "Aunt Eleanor, I'm sorry I said all those things last night. I was angry. But I understand things better now. I can see why you love flying.

23

And I can see that you still love the farm."

"The farm is my home," said Aunt Eleanor. "It's the place I'll always come back to." She patted Molly's leg. "And you know, all those things you said last night helped me understand better how Grammy and Granpa must feel. I'm flying off, and they're left behind with nothing else at all to do but worry."

Just then they turned into the rutted drive and hit a hole so big, Molly was nearly jounced off her seat. "Well," said Molly with a grin. "Not exactly nothing else at all to do."

Grammy and Granpa were on the

porch waiting for them. "Where on earth have you been?" Grammy asked.

"No place on earth," answered Molly. "We were flying! Aunt Eleanor took me up in her plane."

"Eleanor!" exclaimed Granpa. "What were you thinking of, taking the child up in that contraption?"

"Oh, it was wonderful, Granpa!" said Molly. "Aunt Eleanor flew us right over the farm. You should see it from up there. It looks so small and perfect. The farm is Aunt Eleanor's North Star."

"Her what?" asked Granpa, surprised. He and Grammy and Aunt Eleanor looked at Molly with interest.

"The farm is Aunt Eleanor's North

25

Star," Molly said eagerly. "You see, when Dad was about to leave for the war, I was really sad. One night we went outside, and Dad pointed out the North Star. He said that in olden times, sailors used the North Star to guide them because they could always find it. They could trust it to be shining brightly at the end of the Little Dipper."

"How's that like the farm?" asked Granpa.

Molly went on. "Dad said we all need a North Star, something we can find even when we're lost, something we can depend on to be the same no matter where we wander. He said that Mom and Jill and Ricky and Brad and I had to be

his North Star when he went off to the war. Even if he couldn't see us, he'd know we were in place. He'd picture us at home and know we were waiting for him, so he'd never feel lost."

Aunt Eleanor put her arm around Molly's shoulders and gave a little squeeze. "You're right, Molly," she said.

"That *is* how I feel about the farm." She looked at Grammy and Granpa and asked gently, "Will you be my North Star when I go away?"

Grammy's eyes were full of tears. Granpa's voice was sad when he said, "Your mother and I don't want you to go, Eleanor. But we can see you are bound and determined."

"Dad—" Aunt Eleanor began.

Granpa continued. "You do what you feel you have to do," he said. "Your mother and I will be proud to stay here and be your North Star if that will help you come back home to us safe and sound after the war."

Aunt Eleanor hugged him. "Thanks,

Dad," she said. She hugged Grammy, too. Then she turned to Molly and said, "I sure am glad you took that ride with me in the airplane today."

Granpa grinned. "Speaking of rides," he said, "I'm thinking maybe the time has come to smooth those ruts out of the driveway. I'm going to drive to town to get a load of gravel. Anybody want to go for one last bumpy ride with me?"

Molly, Aunt Eleanor, and Grammy laughed out loud. "I do, Granpa," Molly said. And they climbed into the noisy old truck together.

LOOKING BACK

FLYING IN 1944

World War Two was a time when most Americans shared a wish to help

An Air Force pilot in 1943

their country. Children like Molly held scrap drives and bought War Stamps. American men volunteered to fight. They became soldiers, pilots, and sailors. American women filled the office and factory jobs that the men left behind.

Some women, however, wanted to do more than work in an office or factory.

These women were teachers, secretaries, and mothers who shared a love of flying. So, like Molly's Aunt Eleanor, they joined the WASPs, the Women's Airforce Service Pilots.

The WASPs were the first group of women pilots to fly for the armed forces. They were organized in 1942, and Jacqueline Cochran was the director of the pilots.

Jacqueline Cochran was one of the most famous women flyers of her lifetime. She received the trophy for outstanding woman flier in the world

Jacqueline Cochran in her WASP uniform

Jacqueline Cochran in the cockpit of a World War Two fighter plane

three years in a row and set over 200 flying records. She had suggested the idea of an organization of women fliers to First Lady Eleanor Roosevelt in 1939. Together, with the chief of the Army Air Corps, they formed the WASPs three years later.

During World War Two, over 25,000 women applied to be WASPs. Almost 2,000 women were accepted and began training to become pilots.

When the women arrived at the

airfield, they were issued flight gear and a uniform. Because there was not a uniform for women, they had to wear the same thing the men wore, a pair of coveralls.

The coveralls were issued in large men's sizes and were too big for the women pilots. The women nicknamed them "zoot suits." To make them fit,

WASP trainees in their "zoot suits"

women had to roll up the sleeves and pant legs and belt the suits at the waist. They were hard to wash, too. Women wore them in the shower, lathered them up with soap, and scrubbed them with a brush.

The suits had one good thing—a built-in notepad. There was a patch over the right knee that the women used to record their takeoff and landing times.

After seven months of training, more than a thousand of the women graduated and earned their wings. When they graduated, the WASP fliers wore "Fifinella" patches on their jackets. Walt Disney artists designed the fairy

Fifinella was the WASPs' mascot and good-luck charm.

Fifinella. She was supposed to protect the fliers from danger.

WASP pilots didn't fly in foreign countries and weren't allowed to fly in battle. Instead, they flew people and equipment to and from airfields across America.

The women did take risks, though. WASP fliers towed targets behind their planes to help male pilots

WASP pilots returning from a flying mission

practice their shooting. The men used real guns, and accidents did happen. Also, some planes the women pilots tested crashed. In all, 38 WASP fliers died while serving their country.

The women pilots also had a lot to prove. Many men did not believe that women could handle large military planes. One plane, called the P-39, gave the women a chance to show their abilities.

The P-39 Airacobra

Many people called the P-39 a "flying coffin" because of its high accident rate. One general suspected there were accidents because the men who tested the planes weren't flying them according to directions. He decided to let women pilots test the P-39, because they paid more attention in class and always read the directions for any plane they flew.

When the women tested the plane, they had no problems. The general wrote, "They had no trouble, none at all. And I had no more complaints from the men."

The women fliers had fun, too. They sunbathed on the airfields, played Ping-Pong, and organized plays and concerts.

Sunbathing on an airfield

They also sang new words to "The Yankee Doodle Boy":

> *We are Yankee Doodle pilots,*
> *Yankee Doodle, do or die.*
> *Real live nieces of our Uncle Sam*
> *Born with a yearning to fly!*

The Air Force ended the WASP program in 1944, toward the end of the war. For many years, these women pilots were forgotten. It wasn't until 1979 that the WASP fliers were given the same honors that male pilots had received.

Women today enjoy careers as pilots in the Air Force. Their jobs are the same as the men's because of a recent decision: women can now fly in combat.

An Air Force pilot of today

MOLLY AND THE
MOVIE STAR

MOLLY AND THE
MOVIE STAR

Molly McIntire burst into the kitchen running so fast her brown braids stuck straight out behind her. "Guess what!" she exclaimed. "My class is collecting money to buy a War Bond at the big rally a week from Saturday, and *I'm* going to give the money to Melody Moore! Can you believe it?"

"My goodness!" said Mom.

Mrs. Gilford, the housekeeper, asked, "Who's Melody Moore?"

Molly gasped. "You mean you don't know?" she said. "Melody Moore is a *very* famous movie star. She's coming to *our* town. Everybody will come to the rally to see her, and she'll sing and dance and make everybody feel patriotic and happy so they'll buy War Bonds."

"Well," Mrs. Gilford began, "War Bonds are a good thing, but—"

"Oh, I know!" interrupted Molly proudly. "That's how I was chosen to give our money to Melody Moore. I explained War Bonds the best of anyone in my class. I said you buy a War Bond for eighteen dollars and seventy-five cents. The government uses the money to buy things for our

46

soldiers. But the government is really only borrowing the money, because in ten years you can take your War Bond to a bank and get twenty-five dollars for it."

"Very good!" said Mom.

"As I was saying," Mrs. Gilford went on firmly, "War Bonds are good. But I don't see why the rallies have to be flimflam shows, with glamour girls singing and all. People should buy the bonds to help our fighting boys because it's the right thing to do."

"Yes! Well!" said Mom. "How much money are you supposed to bring in, Molly?"

"About a dollar, I guess," said Molly.

"I have fifty cents in my bank I can use."

"And you can use your movie money for tomorrow and next Saturday," added Mom.

"Oh, no," said Molly. "I *have* to go to the movie tomorrow. Melody Moore is in it. I'll *earn* the money I need for the War Bond. I'll put on a show, or paint the garage, or—"

"You can do chores," said Mrs. Gilford. "If you mop the kitchen floor, sort the laundry, polish the silver, and rake the Victory garden, I'd say that would be worth fifty cents."

Molly frowned. Chores were dull. She wanted to do something exciting to earn the money.

But Mom was already saying, "Molly, I'll give you the money Friday if Mrs. Gilford says you've done the chores to her satisfaction."

"Okay," Molly sighed. *Anyway, the chores will be easy*, she thought.

The next day, when Molly went to the movies with her best friends Linda and Susan, she was very glad she had not given up her movie money. Molly loved everything about going to the movies. She and Linda and Susan liked to get to the theater early, buy their tickets, and then walk slowly around the lobby, studying the posters of coming attractions.

They liked to have plenty of time to gaze at the candy in the big glass case. Molly always ended up getting popcorn, but Linda and Susan tried something new each week—candy bars or licorice twists, caramels or taffy. The girls said hi to all their friends from school as they arrived. Almost everyone came to the movies on Saturday afternoon.

This afternoon, Molly settled into her seat as the theater went dark. The curtains parted. The music swelled. As the movie began, Molly shivered with pleasure. There was Melody Moore on the screen, larger than life, wearing a Red Cross nurse's uniform! *Oh*, thought Molly, *I can't wait*

till I meet Melody Moore.

After the movie, the girls walked
to the McIntires' house. "Well, girls.
How was the movie?" Mrs. Gilford asked.

"Melody Moore was great," Molly
said. "She was so brave when she
was taking care of the soldiers in the
field hospital."

51

"I loved it when she and the other nurses sang and danced for the soldiers," said Linda.

All three girls sang the song from the movie: "I'm a soldier in the army of lo-ove . . ."

Mrs. Gilford muttered, "Nurses singing and dancing. Nonsense!"

Susan said, "There's one thing I don't get. Why didn't Melody Moore tell that tall soldier before he left that she loved him? Why did she hide a letter in his sock in his duffel bag?"

"Because!" exclaimed Molly. "You can't go around blabbing to someone that you love him! Hiding the letter in his sock

52

was much more romantic."

"Oh," said Susan. "But that other nurse, the one with fingernail polish, kissed him before he left. I was afraid he was going to fall in love with her instead of Melody Moore."

"Of course not," said Molly. "He loved Melody Moore from the first moment he saw her. He fell in love with her when she did that special salute." Molly tilted her head, winked, saluted, and twirled on her toes.

"Gosh, Molly," said Linda. "You do that salute exactly like Melody Moore!"

"Yes," sighed Susan. "Molly, you are so lucky. I just can't believe you're really, truly going to meet Melody Moore at the rally."

"The point of the rally is to buy War Bonds, *not* to ogle movie stars," said Mrs. Gilford. "Molly hasn't even begun to earn the money she's supposed to give to the War Bond fund."

Molly said quickly, "I'll do the chores, Mrs. Gilford. I'll start tomorrow."

But the next day, Sunday, Susan invited Molly and Linda over to listen to Melody Moore records. So Molly didn't begin her chores until Monday after school. She got off to a bad start.

She tried to rake the leaves out of the Victory garden, but the wind kept blowing them back in. When Mrs. Gilford came to check on her work, Molly said crossly,

"I shouldn't be working outside in this weather. What if I catch a cold? I don't want Melody Moore to see me with a red nose."

"Rake harder," said Mrs. Gilford. "That'll warm you up."

As the days passed, the indoor chores didn't go much better. Mrs. Gilford made Molly polish the silver twice, because it was streaky the first time. Molly had to mop the kitchen floor twice, too, because she forgot to rinse it the first time. *I bet Melody Moore never does housework,* thought Molly. She held the mop as if it were a micro-phone and looked at her reflection in the toaster. "I'm a soldier in the army of lo-ove," she sang.

Molly stopped. Mrs. Gilford was standing in the doorway watching her. "Molly," she said sternly, "the trouble with you is that you are so caught up with your imaginary movie friends, you can't keep your mind on the task before you."

The trouble with Mrs. Gilford is that she has no imagination, Molly thought later. *She only cares about boring things like scrubbing floors. Mrs. Gilford could never be like a heroine in a movie. She could never do anything brave or dramatic. Never.*

On Friday morning, Mom asked, "How did Molly do with the chores,

Mrs. Gilford?" Molly stood still. She was not sure what Mrs. Gilford would say.

"Well," said Mrs. Gilford, "she hasn't sorted the laundry yet."

Mom turned to Molly. "You'll sort the laundry after school, won't you, Molly?"

"Yes," answered Molly.

"Then here's the money you earned," said Mom, handing two quarters to Molly.

"Thanks, Mom," said Molly. She hurried off to school to add her dollar to the War Bond fund. Her teacher, Miss Campbell, replaced all the change with dollar bills. She put the bills in an envelope and handed it to Molly.

"We're trusting you to take care of

this money, Molly," said Miss Campbell. "We're proud that you'll represent us at the War Bond rally."

Molly put the envelope in her book bag and buckled it securely. She held the book bag with both hands as she walked to Susan's house after school. She kept the bag next to her while she and Linda and Susan listened to Melody Moore records. She held it tight as she ran home, just in time for dinner.

Mrs. Gilford met her with a grim look. "You forgot about sorting the laundry."

"Oh!" said Molly. "Whoops! I'm sorry."

"I hope so," said Mrs. Gilford. "I'm

going now. Your sister Jill is in charge until your mother gets home, which will be very late. After dinner, I want you to sort the laundry. Put everything that needs to be mended in the basket. Your mother can drop the mending off at my house tomorrow morning on the way to the rally. She has to go early. I have no wish to go to that circus of a rally myself." Mrs. Gilford tied her scarf under her chin in a tight knot. "It'll do you good to have a task tonight. It'll keep your mind off this Melanie Moon nonsense."

"Melody Moore," said Molly.

"Whatever," said Mrs. Gilford. Then she left.

After dinner, Molly's sister Jill and her brothers Ricky and Brad went into the living room to listen to a radio program. Molly felt rather forlorn in the kitchen all by herself, sorting the clean laundry into piles. Almost all of Ricky's socks went into the mending pile to be darned. Molly wiggled her finger through a hole in the heel of one sock. *It's a good thing the sock Melody Moore hid her love note in didn't have a hole like this,* she thought.

Suddenly, Molly had an inspiration. She could put the War Bond money in a sock and hand the sock to Melody Moore at the rally tomorrow! That way Melody

Moore would know she had seen her movie. And Molly could do her special tilt, wink, salute, and twirl, too. Melody Moore would love it! She would say, "Molly McIntire, you're a star!" Putting the money in a sock was a great idea!

Quickly, Molly ran upstairs with one of Ricky's socks that didn't have a hole. She took the envelope with the money, folded it, and put it in the toe of the sock. It was perfect! It was just like in the movie! Molly stood in front of her mirror and practiced handing the sock to Melody Moore and saluting her special salute over and over. Tilt, wink, salute, twirl. Tilt, wink, salute, twirl. Finally, she put the sock on her chair with her

Putting the money in a sock was a great idea!

clothes, so she would not forget it the next morning. She went to bed humming, "I'm a soldier in the army of lo-ove!"

Molly was too nervous to sleep well. She was half awake when her mother came in to kiss her good night. By the time Molly woke up the next morning, Mom had already left the house.

This is it! thought Molly. *This is the day I meet a movie star!* She jumped out of bed. When she looked at her chair, she froze in horror. The sock! The sock with the money was gone! Frantically, Molly threw everything off the chair. She looked under the chair, under the bed, in the closet, then under the chair again. Nothing.

She ran down the hall into Ricky's room and began tossing socks out of his drawer. "Ricky, wake up!" she shouted. "Did you take one of your socks out of my room last night?"

"No," said Ricky. "What's—" But Molly was already gone.

She flew down the stairs to the kitchen. Jill was sitting at the table, calmly drinking juice. "Jill!" gasped Molly. "Did you take one of Ricky's socks out of my room last night?"

"No," said Jill.

"Where could it be?" wailed Molly. "I hid the money for my class's War Bond in the sock, and now it's gone!"

"What?" exclaimed Jill. "Why did

you put the money in a sock?"

"I wanted it to be like in Melody Moore's movie," said Molly.

Jill sighed. "You and your big ideas," she said. "Well, let's search the house. The sock has to be here somewhere."

Molly and Jill started searching and did not stop until they'd looked in every nook and cranny of the house. Even Ricky and Brad helped them search. Finally, they gave up. The sock was nowhere to be found.

"What am I going to do?" moaned Molly.

"You'll have to go to the rally and explain what happened," said Ricky.

"I can't!" said Molly. "I'd rather

die than tell Melody Moore what I did!"

"Write her a confession note,"
Jill said.

"Yeah," said Ricky. "Hide it in
a sock."

"No!" said Molly and Jill together.

"But what'll I tell my class?" Molly
asked. "They'll all hate me."

"Tell them you'll pay the money
back," said Ricky. "If you don't go to the
movies for two hundred weeks, which is
about four years, you'll have twenty
dollars. Then you can pay back the
money you lost."

"Well," sighed Molly. "After this, I
don't think I'll ever want to go to the
movies again for the rest of my life."

As soon as Molly's note was ready, she and Jill and Brad and Ricky left for the rally. Molly felt as if she were marching to her execution as they walked to the high school football field.

Molly took her seat on the stage that was set up at one end of the field, and looked out at the crowd. She felt hot with shame and cold with fear. She slid her confession note out of her pocket and reread it. *Miss Moore,* it said. *Please don't read this out loud. I lost my class's money. I will pay it back. I am sorry. Your fan, Molly McIntire.*

Just then, the crowd started to murmur. An army jeep stopped at the

edge of the field. Molly held her breath
as the crowd started to cheer. Because
there she was! There was Melody Moore,
smiling and waving and walking through
the crowd. She looked as beautiful as she
did in the movies!

Melody Moore danced up the steps
of the stage and flashed a huge smile.
The crowd whistled and clapped and
yelled. The band played "I'm a soldier
in the army of lo-ove," and everyone
sang along with Melody Moore. Everyone, that is, except Molly. She was too
miserable.

Then Melody Moore held her hands
up for quiet. "I'm so pleased to be here,"
she said. "I know everyone in town wants

to buy a War Bond today, especially the children of Willow Street School. Let's give these kids a hand!"

The crowd clapped and shouted. The band played a drumroll as a cute kindergartner handed an envelope to Melody Moore. The drummer hit the cymbals, and the crowd whooped and whistled when Melody Moore kissed the little first grader who handed her an envelope. Everyone laughed and cheered for the second grader who shook Melody Moore's hand too long. Molly could hardly breathe. Her turn was next! She stood up to walk across the stage toward Melody Moore. The drums began to roll.

The crowd quieted. *If only the world would end now,* Molly thought.

HONK! blasted the horn of the jeep. Molly just about jumped out of her skin. Everyone looked over at the jeep. HONK! HONK! The jeep nosed its way through the crowd, honking wildly. People jostled one another to clear a path. Molly looked and gasped. She could not believe her eyes. It was Mrs. Gilford!

Mrs. Gilford? thought Molly. *What on earth is she doing here?* Mrs. Gilford looked like the fearless general of an invading army. She was standing up in the jeep next to the driver. With one hand she held on to the windshield, and with the other hand she waved something over her head.

"Miss Moon!" Mrs. Gilford called out dramatically. "Stop immediately!"

The jeep pulled up next to the stage, and Mrs. Gilford climbed out. She strode up the steps with determination, nodded briskly to Melody Moore, and said, "Just a moment, Miss Moon." Then she walked straight over to Molly and handed her Ricky's sock. "Your mother picked up this sock by mistake and brought it to my house with the mending," Mrs. Gilford said. "I knew how important it was as soon as I saw it."

Molly was flooded with joy and relief. "Oh, Mrs. Gilford, thank you!" she whispered.

Mrs. Gilford looked like the fearless general of an invading army.

Mrs. Gilford smiled at Molly and gave her a nudge toward Melody Moore. "Go along, now," she said. "Your movie star is waiting."

Molly flew across the stage and handed Melody Moore the sock.

Melody Moore laughed. She pulled the envelope out of the sock, opened it, and waved the money at the crowd. She smiled at Molly.

"I can see that you're a real fan!" she said. "What's your name, sweetheart?"

"Molly McIntire," said Molly.

"Well, thank you, Molly," said Melody Moore. "And thank your grandmother, too."

"Oh, she's not my grandmother,"

said Molly. "That's Mrs. Gilford. She's my . . . she's my friend." *Good old Mrs. Gilford,* Molly thought. *She came to my rescue, just like a heroine in a movie.* Molly smiled at Mrs. Gilford, then turned to Melody Moore. Molly tilted her head, winked, saluted, and twirled on her toes. Melody Moore did the same thing right back, and the audience exploded into applause.

"Molly McIntire," said Melody Moore, "you're a star!"

LOOKING BACK

MOVIES IN 1944

Times were tough for girls growing up during World War Two. They had to do without a lot of things they wanted or needed. Many girls had fathers and brothers fighting overseas. The world was a pretty scary place.

But on Saturdays everything seemed different. Saturday was movie day—the best day of the week. For ten cents each, girls and boys in town could spend the afternoon at the theater. Saturday matinees showed double features!

Walking into the theater lobby was like entering another world. Many theaters were like palaces, with sparkling chandeliers and plush carpeting. Uniformed ushers took tickets. It was grand and exciting.

Even better, the lobbies smelled of lemon drops, Milk Duds, peppermints, and hot popcorn—treats hard to get during wartime. The candy and popcorn cost just five cents.

*Gene Autry and his horse, Champion,
were in many Westerns.*

And that was just the start. Before the double feature, there might be singers and dancers performing in front of the screen. There might be a contest onstage, with free toys as prizes. You could count on seeing a cartoon or a short Western, with plenty of horses and cowboys. You might also get to see an episode in a *serial*, which left you hanging until the next week, when another episode would be shown.

You were allowed to cheer or boo during the show, and even walk around the theater, talking to your friends. Sometimes, though, the feature movie was so glamorous or so sad that no one thought to talk. One week it might be an adventure movie, like *Lassie Come Home*, in which a courageous dog travels miles to be with her master. Another week it

Lassie®

might be a scary science fiction movie about an earth invasion from outer space.

During wartime, many movies were about being in the military. Brave, glamorous soldiers and pilots fought exciting battles against German and Japanese "bad guys." There were

Since You Went Away—
a home-front movie

"home-front movies" too, which showed families just like Molly's learning how to live without brothers and fathers and uncles.

In the intermission between films, theaters showed black-and-white *newsreels,* which reported on the progress of the war. The newsreels showed actual land, air, and sea battles. The mood in the theater would change during the newsreels. Some people would begin to cry. Others shouted at the images of German and Japanese soldiers. And some people were scared. "I felt I was actually there," remembered one girl. Another girl always timed a trip to the bathroom so she would miss seeing the newsreels completely!

At the end of the day, girls went

Newsreel

home to read magazines like *Modern Screen*, which were all about their favorite movie stars. They could even join fan clubs. If they were lucky, a movie star might visit their hometown. During the war many movie stars traveled the country, joining rallies to sell War Bonds, singing in variety shows to help boost people's spirits,

Movie star Shirley Temple in **Modern Screen**

and pitching in however they could to help the war effort.

Movie stars took their roles in the war very seriously. They knew that movies could offer an escape from the troubles of war. But they could also provide encouragement for people on the home front, and even inspire them to join the army or to take war jobs. Most of all, movies helped remind everyone that no matter the hardships, the war was worth fighting.

Movie star Joan Crawford at a War Bond rally

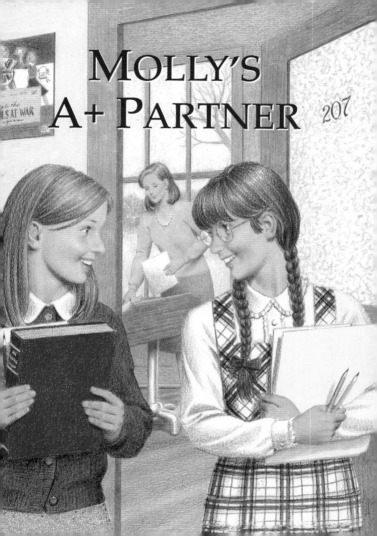

MOLLY'S
A+ PARTNER

207

MOLLY'S
A+ PARTNER

"Susan, this is the best report anyone
has ever done!" said Molly happily.
"I bet we'll get an A+."

"Yes!" agreed Susan as she wrote her
name in fancy script on the cover of the
report. "I'm so glad we did George
Washington and not Abraham Lincoln,
like Linda and Alison. I always think that
tall hat Lincoln wore looks so silly."

Molly chuckled. She didn't see what
Lincoln's hat had to do with anything, but

it didn't matter. Their report was finished, and she was very pleased with it.

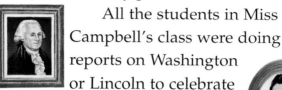

All the students in Miss Campbell's class were doing reports on Washington or Lincoln to celebrate their February birthdays. Molly and Susan were partners, and they had worked very, very hard.

First, they'd marched straight to the library with sharpened pencils, clean white paper, and a special folder neatly labeled "Our Report." Molly read about Washington in the "W" volume of the encyclopedia, and Susan read about him in the "P" volume, under "Presidents." They read books from the biography section, too.

First, they'd marched straight to the library with sharpened pencils, clean white paper, and a special folder neatly labeled "Our Report."

They took notes, and met every day for a week to put their notes together.

When they wrote their first draft, they were careful to write in full sentences, to recheck the facts, and to look up all the hard words in the dictionary. Then Molly copied over the first half of the report in her best handwriting, and Susan copied over the second half. Today at Molly's house they had made a wonderful cover with a drawing of Washington's home, Mount Vernon, on it.

"I'm glad we're partners," Molly said as she signed her name on the cover under Susan's. Both she and Susan felt sorry for Linda. Not that

Alison wasn't nice! It was just that, as Molly went on to say, "It's so lucky when your partner is also one of your good friends."

"Mmm-hmm," Susan murmured vaguely. She was twirling a lock of her hair and staring at a painting in a big art book from the library. "I've been thinking," said Susan, looking up from the book. "You know what would be neat? Instead of just reading our report the way everyone else does, you and I could do something completely different."

"Like what?" asked Molly.

"Well, we could dress up and act out scenes from Washington's life," said Susan. She held up the book to show

Molly. "See? We could make wigs and capes, and—"

"Oh, Susan," said Molly. "I don't think so." Privately, she was horrified. She thought Susan's idea was perfectly terrible! Make wigs? Wear capes? First of all, it was too difficult. Secondly, everyone would laugh! Molly would die of embarrassment to stand up in front of the class in a wig and pretend to be the first president of the United States! "That isn't how you're supposed to present a report," she said. "You're supposed to stand up in your regular clothes and read it aloud to the class."

"Boring," said Susan, pretending to yawn. "Nothing to look at."

"What if we made a timeline showing the most important dates in Washington's life?" suggested Molly.

"That's the kind of thing everyone always does," protested Susan.

"Because that's what you're *supposed* to do," said Molly.

"Then ours will be different," said Susan.

"Then ours will be terrible!" said Molly.

Susan looked stubborn.

Molly sighed. "Listen, Susan. I don't want to do any acting out. I just want to read."

"How about this?" said Susan. "You read, and then you stop at certain points and I'll act something out."

"Well," said Molly slowly. "I *guess* that'll be okay."

"Good!" said Susan. "Then at the end maybe you and I can sing 'Yankee Doodle' together or something."

"*No,*" said Molly flatly. "No singing."

"Okay," said Susan, shrugging, holding up both hands. She grinned at Molly.

"Don't look so worried. It'll be fine.
Really it will."

But Molly couldn't help feeling
worried. She was going to present her
report with a partner who wore a costume
and sang? What had Susan lured her into?

★

As the days went by, Molly worried
more and more. And she began to feel
resentful of Susan, too. After all, as she
was plugging away at making a timeline,
which she was sure would earn them
extra credit, Susan was wasting
her time fussing around trying to
make a tricorn hat, which would
not earn them anything but teasing,

Molly was sure.

The reports were due Wednesday. Tuesday, after school, Molly and Susan met to practice their presentation for the next day. Molly showed Susan the timeline.

"Very nice," said Susan.

Molly's feelings were slightly hurt. She had worked long and hard on her timeline, and she thought Susan should be more enthusiastic. "I notice you didn't bring a costume," she said. "Does that mean you're not going to do that dressing up stuff?"

"Of course I am!" said Susan.

"Then," said Molly sharply, "where's your costume?"

"I couldn't bring it," said Susan. "The cape belongs to my mother, and she didn't

want me dragging it all over the place
and getting it dirty. And I can't move
the hat and the wig because the glue is
too wet."

Molly was nervous. "If I can't see
your costume, can I at least hear what
you're going to say?" she asked.

"Sure!" said Susan. "I've planned it
very carefully." She opened the report. "I'll
draw stars in the margins. Whenever you
come to a star, stop reading because I'm
going to stand up and act something out."

"Okay," said Molly as Susan drew
the stars. "Tell me what you're going to
do at the first star."

"Oh, it'll be great!" said Susan, all
smiles. "I'm going to pretend that I'm

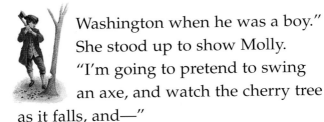 Washington when he was a boy."
She stood up to show Molly.
"I'm going to pretend to swing
an axe, and watch the cherry tree
as it falls, and—"

"Just a second!" Molly interrupted,
sputtering. "I don't think you should do
that cherry tree thing, Susan! Everyone
knows it's probably not true."

"But that's not the point," said
Susan. "I'm going to say—"

Molly interrupted again. "Please don't
do it, Susan!" she begged. "Everyone will
laugh! And Miss Campbell will think we
didn't check our facts! I couldn't stand it!
Not after all my hard work!"

"*Your* hard work?" said Susan.

"I worked hard, too. I'm your partner, remember?"

Humph! Some partner! thought Molly. *Fussing around wasting time on a silly hat!* She said quickly, "I'm just afraid it's going to make us look dumb."

"Dumb?!" exclaimed Susan, her cheeks pink with anger. "Well! If that's the way you feel about it, then I'm not going to tell you the other things I planned to say. I'm going home!"

"Wait!" wailed Molly as Susan stood up. "You can't go!"

But it was too late. The door slammed. Susan was gone.

That night, when Molly's mom came up to tuck her into bed, Molly was wide awake and fretting. "What's the matter?" asked Mom.

Molly sat up. "Susan and I had a fight about our report," she said. "Susan wants to act out parts of it, which I really, really don't like. And she's wasted a lot of time fussing over costumes and stuff that I think is useless. Then today, when she started to tell me what she was going to do, I got upset and she got mad and stormed off."

Mom sighed. "Partnerships can be hard," she said. "Especially when the partners have different ways of doing things."

Mom sighed. "Partnerships can be hard," she said.
"Especially when the partners have different ways of doing things."

"Susan hasn't been a good partner on this report at all," grumbled Molly.

"She worked as hard as you did on the written part of the report, didn't she?" asked Mom.

"Yes," Molly grudgingly admitted.

"And she's been a good friend for a long time, too," added Mom. "I do think it would be too bad if your partnership ended your friendship." She kissed Molly's forehead. "Now try to get some sleep. Good night."

After Mom left, Molly thought about what she'd said. *Mom's right,* she decided. *Susan is a good friend even if she isn't a good partner. Tomorrow I'll tell Susan I'm sorry about the fight.*

Molly went to sleep feeling better, even though she was still sure she was heading toward one of the most embarrassing days of her life.

"Who would like to go first?" asked Miss Campbell the next day.

Linda and Alison shot their hands up, and Miss Campbell chose them to begin.

Molly leaned her chin on her hands and listened as Linda read aloud. Once in a while, Alison held up a picture to illustrate what Linda was reading. *Just exactly the way you're supposed to present a report,* Molly thought wistfully. *Wait'll they get a load of Susan!* She sighed, and remembered her decision to apologize.

Carefully, she slipped a note to Susan.

Susan smiled and sent a note back.

Molly read Susan's note. "Me, too," she said to herself.

"Very nice!" said Miss Campbell when Linda and Alison were done. "You girls worked hard, and you've given us a good, solid report. Molly and Susan, you can go next."

With a sinking heart, Molly went forward. She tacked up her timeline and stood next to Miss Campbell's desk. Susan was crouched behind the desk with her costume in a bag.

Molly began to read: "George Washington, The Father of Our Country. George Washington was born on February 22, 1732." Molly pointed to the beginning of her timeline, and the class murmured appreciatively. *I knew the timeline was a good idea!* Molly thought.

She continued reading: "Washington's father was a wealthy planter. George grew up . . . " As she read, Molly could hear Susan rattling around, putting on her costume. All too soon, Molly came to the first star, which marked the point where she was supposed to stop reading. She stopped. *Here goes!* she thought, bracing herself for giggles.

Susan stood up with a dramatic flourish.

"Oooohh!" gasped all the students admiringly. Molly looked. Her jaw dropped in amazement.

Susan's costume was fantastic! She had a big, sweeping black cape and tall black boots. She'd tucked her pants into the boots to look like breeches. Best of all, on her head she wore a wig made out of cotton balls topped by a gorgeous tricorn hat that was edged in gold braid and decorated with a plume of feathers.

Susan spoke. "There's a story that says that when Washington was a boy, he chopped down his father's best cherry tree." Susan swung an invisible axe, held her hand above her eyes, and pretended to watch a tree fall. "When his father asked him about it, young George supposedly said, 'I did it, Father. I cannot tell a lie.' Well, we don't know if this story is true or not. But the story shows that Washington was famous for being honest, and that's why people trusted him. And the story is also why we have cherry pie on his birthday!"

All the kids laughed and clapped.

Hey, they sort of like this, Molly realized. She went back to reading from the report, pointing to her timeline whenever she mentioned an important date. "George Washington was a famous soldier," she read. "He was the leader of the army at

the time of the American Revolution."
She came to another star, so she stopped,
and Susan spoke again.

"This is a famous painting of
Washington crossing the Delaware River
on Christmas night in 1776," said Susan.
She held up an art book and showed the
class the painting. "He'd mostly lost
battles till then, but in this painting he's
on his way to surprise and, though he
doesn't know it, defeat the British army.
The painting shows him standing up in
the boat like this." Susan struck a proud
pose. "Well, he probably would have
fallen overboard if he really had stood
up in the boat like that! But I think the
artist wanted to show that Washington

Susan struck a proud pose.

was brave, and that's why his soldiers felt good about following him."

"Ahh," said the class, with understanding.

Boy, they really like this, Molly thought. She looked over at Susan and grinned, and then she read again. She came to another star after she read, "During the harsh, cold winter of 1777, George Washington stayed with his soldiers at Valley Forge and suffered just as they did."

Susan had pulled on mittens and a scarf. She had sprinkled powder on her cape to look like snow, and she was carrying sticks of wood. "When Washington stayed with his men, it

112

showed everyone that he was humble,"
she said. "He didn't act the way the
king did. People knew he would be a
good president because he would be
a responsible leader who cared about
them, like a father."

The class nodded and agreed.

Molly read to the end of the report:
"And so you can see, George Washington
was not only our first president, he was
also one of our greatest presidents.
That's why we call him the Father of
Our Country."

Susan added, "George Washington
will always be a well-loved president. You
may not know it, but there is a verse about
him in a song we all sing." Susan sang all

by herself to the tune of "Yankee Doodle":

There was Captain Washington,
Upon a slapping stallion,
A-giving orders to his men,
I guess there was a million.

Molly joined in with everyone else as Susan led them in the chorus:

Yankee Doodle, keep it up,
Yankee Doodle dandy!
Mind the music and the step,
And with the girls be handy!

"Hurray!" cheered the class. They clapped and stamped their feet and whistled.

"That was splendid!" exclaimed

114

Miss Campbell after the class quieted
down. "Molly and Susan, you showed
us how good partners work!" She beamed
at the girls. "A+ for both of you," she said.

Molly smiled at Susan, and Susan
grinned back. Susan's hat was tilted and
her wig was askew, but she didn't look
funny to Molly. She looked like a good
friend—and a very good partner.

LOOKING BACK

FINDING HOPE
IN THE PAST

To celebrate the birthdays of past presidents Washington and Lincoln, Molly's class wrote reports, just as you might do today. For children on the home front during World War Two, remembering Washington and Lincoln was especially important. Both were

George Washington

Abraham Lincoln

leaders during times of war in American history— Washington commanded the Continental troops during the Revolutionary War, and Lincoln was president during the Civil War. And both led their followers to victory.

Remembering past victories gave Americans hope during World War Two. In a radio speech in 1942, President Roosevelt compared the crisis of World War Two to the struggle Americans faced during the Revolutionary War. Many people believed America would never win independence

Roosevelt gave frequent radio speeches.

from England, but Washington and the Continental army proved them wrong. President Roosevelt assured Americans that though they again faced difficult times, victory would be theirs.

Molly and Susan's report touched on one of the most famous events of the Revolutionary War—Washington's crossing of the Delaware River on Christmas night, 1776. Until then, Washington had lost every major battle against the British. He had lost forts, gunpowder, and cannon—and especially men.

A Revolutionary War cannon

The men who remained in Washington's army were cold, hungry, and discouraged. They had begun to lose faith in Washington, and some of his officers even whispered about replacing him.

A soldier's meal: biscuits, hard cheese, and dried beef

The British now occupied New York City. They had declared the war over during the winter because of the bad weather and because they believed Washington's army was no longer a threat to them. The British officers were enjoying themselves, dining on the best food and wine and dancing in ballrooms.

Christmas night found Washington and his men on the bank of the Delaware River. Ice flowed by on the swift current. Sleet stung his face. Winds snared his cape.

Washington encouraged his troops as they struggled across the Delaware River.

His men had no shoes and were hungry. The horses were shoeless, too. They slipped in the ice as they pulled wagons loaded with cannon to the riverbank. The British might have stopped fighting for the winter, but Washington saw this night

as his last chance. He hoped to catch the enemy troops by surprise.

Across the river in Trenton, New Jersey, were Hessians (HESHens). They were soldiers from Germany, hired by King George to fight for England. If Washington could beat the Hessians, he might still win the war. If he failed, all might be lost. The mission's password showed how desperate Washington felt. It was "Liberty or Death."

A spy in Washington's camp wrote a note to the Hessian general in Trenton, telling him that Washington planned to attack at dawn the next day. But the general was attending a Christmas party. He did not want to be bothered. "They're half-naked," he said. "Let them come."

And come they did. At eight o'clock on December 26, after a long, cold night, Washington's troops marched into Trenton. Most of the Hessian soldiers were still in bed, recovering from the party the night before. By nine o'clock, Washington's Continental army had

The surrender of the Hessians at the Battle of Trenton

taken the city and nearly a thousand Hessian prisoners. The Hessian general who had ignored the warning of Washington's attack died in battle that morning. In his pocket was the spy's folded, forgotten note. Washington's desperate mission had succeeded.

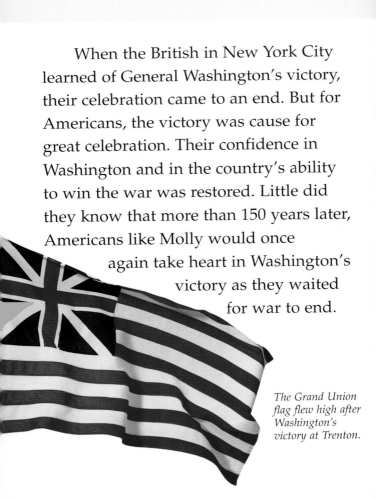

When the British in New York City learned of General Washington's victory, their celebration came to an end. But for Americans, the victory was cause for great celebration. Their confidence in Washington and in the country's ability to win the war was restored. Little did they know that more than 150 years later, Americans like Molly would once again take heart in Washington's victory as they waited for war to end.

The Grand Union flag flew high after Washington's victory at Trenton.

By the 1940s, America's flag had changed, but the country's determination and enthusiasm for victory remained the same.

MOLLY'S
PUPPY TALE

MOLLY'S
PUPPY TALE

Molly McIntire and her two best
friends, Linda and Susan, were
hurrying to Molly's house after school on
a sunny afternoon in May. They couldn't
wait to play with Molly's puppy, Bennett.

"You are so lucky, Molly," sighed Susan.
"I wish I had a dog of my very own,
especially one like Bennett. He's *adorable*."

"He's smart, too," said Linda. "He'll be
like Lassie, probably, when he grows up."

Molly smiled. She believed Linda and

Susan were absolutely right. Bennett was the cutest and smartest puppy in the world. She loved everything about him, from his soft black nose to his always wagging tail. He was lively and cuddly and full of affection. "Bennett already knows his name," Molly told her friends. "This morning he ran straight to me when I called him."

"Gosh!" said Susan. "That *is* smart for a puppy. You've only had him since your birthday in April."

"Most nights I put his basket right on the bed next to me so he won't feel lonely," said Molly.

"Oh, that's so sweet!" said Susan.

"Do you ever get tired of taking care of

him?" asked Linda, who liked to ask practical questions.

"Oh, no," said Molly. "I'd do anything for Bennett. I love him. And he loves me best of anyone in the world."

When the girls got to Molly's house, they said hello to Mrs. Gilford, the McIntires' housekeeper. She was working in her Victory garden, turning over the earth to get it ready for spring planting. Ricky was outside, too, playing tug-of-war with Bennett. Ricky was holding on to one end of an old rag, and Bennett's jaws were clamped on to the other end. Bennett was tossing his head, growling,

133

and wagging his tail wildly.

Molly hardly recognized the muddy, frisky dog as her sweet, cuddly puppy. She felt a little pinch of annoyance. Bennett was clearly having a great time—without her.

"Bennett!" she called. "Here, boy! Come here, Bennett!"

Bennett did not even glance her way.

Molly clapped her hands and whistled. "Bennett! Come!" she called, a little louder this time. "Come here now!"

Bennett ignored her.

Now Molly was more than annoyed. She had just bragged to Linda and Susan about how much Bennett loved her, and now Ricky was making it look as if Bennett liked *him* better than he liked *her!*

Ricky didn't notice the frown on Molly's face. "Hey, look at this!" he said. "I taught Bennett how to fetch a ball." He tossed the ball past Molly. "Go get it, boy!" he said to Bennett.

Bennett bounded after the ball. But before he got to it, Molly snatched him up in her arms. "Just look at him," she said to Ricky crossly. "You've gotten him all muddy."

"And you tired him out," Susan accused.

"And he was having so much fun with you, he didn't pay attention when Molly called him," added Linda, pointing out the exact thing Molly had hoped no one else had noticed.

"A little mud won't hurt him," said Ricky. "Bennett's not a baby anymore. He wants to rough-and-tumble with me. He likes it. And it's good for him."

"*I'll* decide what's good for him," said Molly sharply. "He's *my* puppy." Bennett squirmed in her arms, trying to get down. Molly tightened her grip, turned her back on Ricky, and marched into the house. Linda and Susan followed her, leaving behind whatever else Ricky had to say.

That night, Molly put Bennett's basket right next to her pillow. Bennett licked her face with his rough tongue,

then nestled down and fell asleep. Molly
fell asleep, too, with her hand on his warm
little head.

In the middle of the night, Molly woke
up. She peeked into the basket to be sure
Bennett was sleeping peacefully.

Bennett was gone.

Molly sat up, switched on her lamp, and
put on her glasses. "Bennett?" she said
anxiously. "Bennett?" Quickly, she looked
under the beds, behind the chair, under
her dressing table, and even in the closet.
Bennett was nowhere to be found.

"Bennett!" Molly whispered. "Where
are you?"

Molly tiptoed out into the hall. Ricky's
door was open, so she peered into his

room. There was Bennett, curled up at the foot of Ricky's bed, his sweet, sleeping face resting on his paws.

Molly's heart sank. Could it be that Bennett really *was* beginning to like Ricky more than he liked her? Right then and there, she made up her mind that she would not share Bennett with Ricky at all anymore. She scooped the puppy up off Ricky's bed, carried him back to her room, and put him in his basket. She was careful to close her bedroom door so that it was shut tight.

The next morning, Molly came down late to breakfast. She felt cranky and out of

*There was Bennett, curled up at the foot of Ricky's bed,
his sweet, sleeping face resting on his paws.*

sorts as she let Bennett out the back door.

"You're too late for pancakes," said Mrs. Gilford. She was at the sink, watering seedlings she'd nursed along through the winter for her Victory garden. "It'll have to be cornflakes. Get yourself a bowl."

Ricky jumped up from the table. "I'll feed Bennett," he said.

"No, you will *not*," said Molly.

"What's eating you?" asked Ricky. "I'm just trying to do you a favor."

"Well, I don't need any favors from you," said Molly as she poured too much milk on her cornflakes. "I can take care of Bennett all by myself. You will not do *anything* with him *anymore.* That's final."

An unhappy look crossed Ricky's face. Then he shrugged. "Fine with me, Miss Selfish," he said. He grabbed his schoolbooks and slammed out the door.

Molly ate her soggy cornflakes in silence. When she went to the sink to rinse out her bowl and fix Bennett's breakfast, Mrs. Gilford spoke to her.

"If you ask me, that dog is being mollycoddled. He's not a helpless little ball of fur anymore," she said. "Soon he'll reach the chewing stage, and nothing will be safe. Mark my words, you'll have to keep your eye on him every minute. And he's going to need exercise and training, too. If you're smart, you'll let your brother Ricky help you."

"I don't need his help!" Molly said. "Bennett is my dog, and I will be responsible for him."

Mrs. Gilford raised her eyebrows. "Very well," she said. "But remember, you might be able to keep Bennett out of trouble, but there's no way you can keep him from liking other people. You can pen up a dog, but you can't pen up his affections. It isn't right, and anyway, it's impossible."

Molly did not want to hear any more. She put Bennett in his pen, fed him, kissed him, and hurried off to school.

For the next week or so, Molly had no trouble taking care of Bennett all by herself. He seemed happy to spend the day in his pen snoozing. Molly played with him when she came home from school, and he usually fell asleep at her feet while she was doing her homework in her room after dinner.

But as time passed, taking care of Bennett became more of a problem. One day, Molly stayed after school for Girl Scouts and came home later than usual. Bennett went crazy barking as soon as he saw her. He scrabbled wildly with his paws in the dirt. When Molly opened his pen, he bolted past her! He scooted under the hedge and ran off down the block.

"Bennett!" Molly yelled as she chased after him. "Bennett! Come back!"

But Bennett seemed to think it was great fun to have Molly chasing him and shouting at him. Molly couldn't grab hold of him until he stopped to scatter the neighbors' newspaper all over their lawn.

"Now why'd you run off like that?" Molly asked Bennett as she carried him home. "I guess you were tired of being in your pen." Molly knew the puppy had never been left alone for such a long time before. Ricky used to play with him on Girl Scout days. Molly realized that from now on, she'd have to come straight home from school to care for Bennett.

And that's exactly what Molly did. But even so, the next few weeks were difficult. If Molly took her eyes off Bennett for one second, he got into mischief. He tracked mud across the kitchen floor that Mrs. Gilford had just washed. He grabbed Linda's bag lunch and ate it in one gulp. He chewed up a letter from Dad that Mom had not even read yet.

Molly had to admit that Ricky and Mrs. Gilford had been right about one thing. Now that Bennett was older, he *was* a lot friskier. It was no longer enough just to cuddle and baby him. Molly realized that he needed to be more active. So she began to throw sticks for Bennett to fetch. She played tug-of-war with Bennett and took him for long walks on his leash. Bennett loved his walks. He sniffed enthusiastically at every tree, bush, and pole and barked a friendly hello to every person they passed.

Of course, all of this new exercise took up most of Molly's free time. Some days she felt as if *she* were the one on a leash. But Molly was determined not to share her dog. She was still convinced that she could do everything for Bennett. He did not need anyone else but her.

As Molly and Bennett set forth on their walk one day, Bennett stopped suddenly. He barked eagerly and wagged his tail hard.

"What is it, Bennett?" Molly asked. Then she saw. It was Ricky. He was in the driveway shooting baskets. Bennett strained at the leash, trying to get to him.

"No, Bennett," said Molly quickly. She tried to drag him away for their walk, but he refused to go. Finally, Molly picked him up. He squirmed in her arms, whining and wiggling, struggling to get down.

Molly decided to bring him up to her room and play with him there. She felt a little guilty because no matter what she did to amuse him, he kept scratching at the door, begging to go out. He didn't give up until the sound of the basketball bouncing on the driveway had stopped.

By then, Bennett had worn himself out. Molly left him asleep in his basket when she went to dinner. When she came back upstairs to do her homework, she could not believe her eyes.

"Oh, Bennett!" she gasped. It looked as if it had snowed in her room. Bennett had ripped open her pillow and scattered the feathers everywhere! He had eaten several chapters of her arithmetic workbook, chewed the sleeve off her best blouse, and gnawed on the handle of her book bag.

Worst of all, he had ripped the heads off her precious princess paper dolls.

"Bennett, you are a very bad dog!" scolded Molly. Bennett just looked up at her with his big soft eyes. Molly grimly set to work cleaning up the mess.

After school a few days later, Linda asked, "Want to come over to my house and jump rope with Susan and me?"

Molly hesitated. She knew Bennett was waiting for her. But it was such a beautiful spring day! And it had been so long since she had had an afternoon off from dog duty. Surely Bennett couldn't do any harm while he was safely in his pen.

"Well, I guess it would be okay for just a little while," she said at last.

Jumping rope was fun, and Molly stayed longer than she'd meant to. When she got home, Bennett met her at the end of the driveway, grinning a slobbery

doggy grin and looking very pleased
with himself.

"How did you get out of your pen?"
Molly asked him. She sighed with exas-
peration when she saw that Bennett had
dug an enormous hole and had made
himself an escape tunnel out of his pen.

"Bad dog!" Molly said sternly. "You
shouldn't have dug like that!"

Bennett didn't look the least bit sorry.
He barked happily and scampered off
to play.

While Molly was kicking the dirt back
into the hole Bennett had dug, she happened to look over at Mrs. Gilford's Victory
garden. Her jaw dropped. She walked
toward the garden, staring in dismay.

151

The seedlings Mrs. Gilford had tended so long and transplanted so lovingly had been yanked out of the ground. Bulbs were dug up and gnawed. The seed-packet labels that used to stand so proudly at the end of every row were torn and scattered. Even the rocks Mrs. Gilford had lined up around the edges of the garden had been knocked every which way. All of Mrs. Gilford's careful work was ruined. It had been torn apart by the paws and jaws of Bennett.

Molly knelt, defeated and miserable, in the dirt at the edge of what used to be the Victory garden.

"Looks pretty bad," said Ricky. He was standing behind her.

*Molly knelt, defeated and miserable, in the dirt
at the edge of what used to be the Victory garden.*

153

"Yeah," said Molly.

"Mrs. Gilford's going to be mad," said Ricky.

"Yeah," said Molly again.

"You know," Ricky went on, "today is Friday. Mrs. Gilford won't be back until Monday morning. We could clean up this mess and get a good start at replanting everything by Monday if we worked at it this weekend."

"You'd help me?" Molly asked. She couldn't believe her ears.

"Yeah, well, you'd have to pay me back somehow," said Ricky.

"How?" asked Molly. She was suspicious, but she was desperate, too.

"Bennett," said Ricky quickly. "Let me

154

play with him and teach him stuff and help take care of him."

Molly didn't answer. Just then, Bennett ran to her with something in his mouth. He stood in front of her wagging his tail so hard, his whole rear end was moving. He nudged her with his head and wriggled with joy when she hugged him. *Oh, Bennett,* Molly thought, *I love you so much.* Molly knew Bennett loved her, too. But she realized that sharing Bennett with Ricky was the right thing for the puppy— and for her.

"Okay," she said to Ricky. "It's a deal."

"Good," said Ricky. He sat next to Molly and said to Bennett, "Here, boy!"

Bennett jumped up on Ricky, smearing

dirt all over his shirt. Then he jumped on
Molly and dropped what he had in his
mouth so that he could lick her face.

Molly looked down at her lap and saw
one of Mrs. Gilford's gardening gloves.
Bennett had chewed off all the fingers.
Molly grinned. She held the glove up to

show Ricky and said, "You can start
sharing Bennett right now. I think he's
been mollycoddled long enough!"

LOOKING BACK

DOGS IN 1944

During World War Two, dogs played an important role in the war effort—both at home and overseas. On the home front, dogs were loving, lively companions who kept their owners' spirits up. Girls and boys who were responsible for caring for a pet—especially a mischievous puppy like Bennett—had less time to worry about the war.

Even children without pets found comfort in America's favorite furry movie star, Lassie. In the

1943 movie *Lassie Come Home*, the collie is separated from the people she loves and will stop at nothing to find her way back to them. Many children during World War Two knew just how Lassie felt. They, too, were separated from family members—those fighting the war overseas. Perhaps Lassie gave children hope that their loved ones would soon find their way home.

Lassie®

Soldiers and sailors missed their dogs back home.

Some dogs did more than cheer up people on the home front. Between 1942 and 1945, the United States military trained thousands of dogs to work alongside soldiers in the heat of battle. Some worked as guard dogs, others as messengers, and still others as rescue dogs that brought help to wounded soldiers.

Most of the dogs in the military were family pets volunteered by their owners. People with smart, obedient dogs were proud to sign them up for service because it was another way to help the war effort. But not all dogs could become soldiers. Dogs had to weigh at least fifty pounds, be at least twenty inches tall, and be between the ages of one and five. Small dogs like Bennett weren't accepted because it was thought that the enemy wouldn't fear them!

Dogs "signed" their application forms with pawprints.

German shepherds, on the other hand, were natural soldiers. Because of their keen senses, intelligence, and steady nerves, they were the most popular breed in the military. Many other large dogs—from Dobermans to

Dalmatians—joined the service, too.

All dogs that entered the service had to go through basic training. Handlers taught the dogs simple commands like "heel," "sit," "down," "stay," and "come." After basic training, dogs learned more advanced skills, like crawling low to the ground or through barbed wire, climbing up ramps, and jumping over obstacles.

Crawling was usually the first war skill that dogs learned.

The hardest lesson for most dogs, though, was learning not to fear gunfire.

To train dogs, handlers rewarded them with praise and a pat on the head for what

Some dogs even learned to parachute!

was done right—not punishment for what was done wrong. And because dogs learn best from each other, handlers enlisted the help of more experienced dogs when training the new "recruits."

Sentry dogs helped the Coast Guard protect beaches on the home front.

Many dogs were trained to work as *sentry*, or guard, dogs. Because of their sharp senses, dogs were able to warn their handlers if the enemy was nearby. Sentry dogs were especially helpful at night, when most attacks happened. If a sentry dog smelled or heard a stranger approaching, the dog would bark or growl to alert its handler. Other dogs called *scouts* learned to warn their handlers silently so that the enemy wouldn't hear the barking and be able to escape.

166

Dogs trained as *messengers* carried important information back and forth between two handlers. Maps and letters were placed in metal tubes that were attached to the dogs' collars. If a troop of soldiers was cut off from its command post, the soldiers could send a messenger dog to get help or information about where the enemy was.

A messenger dog receives his mission.

Messenger dogs swam rivers, climbed walls, and crawled through barbed wire—anything to complete their missions. Dogs made good messengers because they could run much faster than men and were lower to the ground, so they were less likely to be seen or shot. Still, many messenger dogs were wounded while on the job. Dick, a black

No wall was too high for this dog to climb!

Labrador retriever, was shot in the back and shoulder while running through enemy territory. He didn't stop running until he had delivered his message. Then, safely back with his handler, Dick died from his wounds.

Human soldiers who were wounded on the battlefield were sometimes helped by another group of military dogs called *rescuers*. Rescue dogs were trained to find wounded soldiers and keep them awake—and alive—until nurses could reach them. And *pack dogs*, which were usually larger

Rescue dogs wore the Red Cross symbol.

*Rescue dogs—with first-aid kits strapped to their backs—
practice leaping over obstacles to get to wounded soldiers.*

breeds like Great Danes and Saint
Bernards, carried medical supplies,
food, and water to soldiers in need.

When the war ended, dogs in the
military were considered true heroes.
These four-footed soldiers had saved
many lives and even may have helped
to shorten the war. But now it was time to

return to their families at home. Military dogs were trained to go back to civilian life, and by 1947, every volunteer dog had been returned to its owner. Imagine how children felt when they were reunited with their pets after so many years!

MOLLY
MARCHES ON

MOLLY
MARCHES ON

Molly McIntire ran up the path to her
tent as fast as her legs could carry
her. She flung back the tent flap and
announced, "We're going! Tomorrow's
the day! All the new campers are going
on the overnight nature hike!"

"Hurray!" shrieked Linda and Susan,
Molly's best friends, who were also new
campers.

"You lucky ducks," sighed their tent-
mate, Irene. She had been at camp before,

so she was an old camper. "I wish I could go on that hike again."

"I can't wait!" exclaimed Molly. Ever since she had arrived at Camp Gowonagin one week ago, the old campers had been telling her about the overnight nature hike. It was the first hike of the summer, so that alone made it exciting. But what made it extra special was this: there was a surprise at the end. Old campers were sworn to secrecy about it. "We can't tell you what the surprise is," they'd say. "But, oh! You'll love it!"

Molly often daydreamed about what the surprise might be. A cave? A lake? An eagle's nest? To Molly the surprise was all the more wonderful because you had to earn it. It was a discovery to be found only at the end of a long, hard hike. No one was going to give the surprise away, so Molly didn't ask questions about it. She was enchanted with the mystery of it all.

But Linda liked to get to the bottom of things. "This surprise business is for the birds," she was saying to Irene. "Couldn't you at least give us a hint?"

Irene just grinned.

"I hope it doesn't have to do with canoes," said Susan nervously. "We don't have to paddle up a waterfall or anything, do we?"

Irene giggled. "I can't tell you what the surprise is," she said. "But, oh! You'll love it."

Molly was sure she would.

In fact, Molly was sure she was going to love the whole overnight nature hike more than any other girl at Camp Gowonagin. She had been looking forward to being in the woods for so long! Back home, before she came to camp, Molly had read a book about Sacagawea, the Shoshone Indian woman who helped the explorers Lewis and Clark on their journey through the wilderness, across the Rocky Mountains, and to the Pacific Ocean in 1805. Molly thought Sacagawea was the bravest, smartest, most admirable person she had ever heard of.

On the nature hike, I will be just like

Sacagawea, Molly thought as she packed her rucksack. *I'll walk silently through the woods. I'll sleep under the stars. I'll cook over a campfire. And when I reach the surprise, I'll be just like Sacagawea finding the Pacific Ocean with Lewis and Clark. Oh, if Sacagawea could see me tomorrow, I know she'd be proud!*

"We're from Gowonagin, and no one could be prouder, and if you cannot hear us, we'll yell a little louder!"

"Louder?" muttered Molly crossly. Ever since they'd left camp at sunrise that morning, all the other hikers had been yowling stupid songs at the tops of their lungs. They screeched at vines that looked like snakes. They stamped on sticks to snap them.

Everyone, including her own friends Linda and Susan, was ruining the nature hike for Molly. They were *supposed* to be moving silently, swiftly through the woods, without disturbing so much as a leaf. Instead, they were crashing through the woods like a herd of stampeding elephants! Molly knew this was not the way true woodspeople conducted themselves. She was sure Sacagawea would be horrified.

Even Miss Butternut, the counselor who was leading the hike, was acting all wrong. She tooted on her bugle to get the girls' attention, and then she began speaking in her loud fluty voice as if they

*Everyone was ruining the nature hike for Molly. They were **supposed** to be moving silently, swiftly through the woods.*

were all back in the Mess Hall at camp!

"Girls," she said. "Observe these stones placed in the shape of an arrowhead. These stones point out our way." A little later she asked, "Girls, can anyone tell me what this stick supported by two other sticks means?"

Susan, whose sister was a Girl Scout, piped up with the answer. "That means it's two more miles to the end of the trail," she said.

"Splendid, Susan!" Miss Butternut said, beaming. "Now, girls, do you see the berry stain on the trunk of this tree?"

Molly didn't pay much attention while Miss Butternut talked loudly on and on about different trail marks. Molly thought sticks and stones and berry juice on trees were for babies. Sacagawea certainly didn't have any such trail marks to follow in the wilderness. Oh, no! Sacagawea had to rely on the shadows cast by the trees, the scent of water in the air, and the sound of the wind to find *her* way. Molly started to pretend that she was Sacagawea. She took some deep breaths.

"What are you doing?" asked Susan. She and Linda were walking behind Molly.

"I'm smelling the air like Sacagawea did," said Molly.

"What for?" asked Susan.

"To find the way," said Molly shortly.

"You're kidding," said Linda. "That's silly. You can just follow the trail marks, for Pete's sake."

But Susan took a deep breath, too. "Do you smell wienies?" she asked Molly. "I'm sort of hoping the surprise is that someone is cooking lunch for us. I hope it's wienies!"

Linda laughed. "Wienies? That's not what hikers eat." She began to sing, "Great green gobs of greasy grimy gopher guts . . ."

"Cut it out!" said Molly, annoyed. But Linda just sang louder, and soon the other hikers were singing with her. Molly was glad when Miss Butternut blew her bugle and all the hikers stopped singing and came to a halt.

"Well, girls, this is it," said Miss Butternut. "This is where the race to the surprise begins." She waited for the girls' cheers to die down before she went on. "I will now divide you into two teams. Each team has its own marked trail to follow. At the end of your trail, you'll find the surprise. You'll know when you get there because the surprise is . . . well, I can't tell you what it is, but—"

"We'll love it!" all the hikers shouted together.

"Yes!" said Miss Butternut with a laugh. "And lunch is there, too."

Quickly, Miss Butternut divided the hikers into teams. Molly, Linda, and Susan were on a team with five girls they didn't know very well.

"Now, before you go," said Miss Butternut, "let's recite the three rules of hiking."

Rules! thought Molly. *Sacagawea didn't need rules any more than she needed trail marks.* But all the other girls spoke together: "Never hike alone. Stay on the marked trail. Carry water."

"Splendid!" said Miss Butternut. "Very well, off you go! See you at the surprise."

"Hurray!" the girls yelled as they set forth into the woods.

Molly walked fast so that she was well ahead of the rest of her noisy team. After a short while, she came to a place where the trail split in two. Molly never stopped. She forged ahead on the branch of the trail that led steeply downhill. The rest of the team stopped at the split.

"Hey, Molly!" Linda shouted after her. "You're going the wrong way!"

Molly walked back to the split. "No, I'm not," she said.

"Yes, you are," said Susan. "The trail goes uphill. See that stick pointing the way?"

"That's just an old stick that fell off a tree," said Molly. "Anybody can see that the bigger trail goes downhill. That uphill trail is just a deer path or something."

"No, it's not—" Susan began.

*"The trail goes uphill," said Susan. "See that
stick pointing the way?"*

"Let's not waste time arguing," cut in Linda. "Everyone who wants to go downhill, follow Molly. Everyone who wants to go uphill, follow me."

Molly turned sharply and marched down the steep path. No one followed her.

"You're breaking the first rule of hiking," Susan called after her.

"I don't care!" Molly shouted back. And she didn't. Now at last she could *really* feel like Sacagawea, alone in the quiet woods. Down, down, down Molly walked. She was proud of the way she moved smoothly and placed her feet gently so she did not make any noise.

The trail grew narrower each step of the way. It crossed Molly's mind that they'd hiked uphill all morning, so it was a little funny that she was going steadily downhill now. And she did wish the trail weren't getting so hard to follow. After an hour of hiking alone, she was only guessing where the trail was.

Molly stopped to decide which way to go. She heard a bird whistling, and leaves rustling, and—with shock, Molly heard the thump of heavy footsteps and the crackling sound of a large creature push-ing through the underbrush. Molly's heart beat fast. Was it a bear? Was it a bobcat? She looked around frantically for a tree to climb.

"Molleee!" a voice called. "Molly! Where are you?"

Molly let out her breath. That was no bear. That was Susan. "I'm over here!" she shouted.

Susan emerged from the trees, red-faced and sweaty. "I couldn't let you break the first rule of hiking," she panted.

Molly didn't want to admit it, but she was quite glad to see her friend. "How'd you find me?" she asked.

"Gosh, I don't know," said Susan. "I think you must have broken the second rule of hiking, too. That's the one about staying on the marked trail. I haven't seen any trail marks for miles." Susan plopped down on a rock. "I hope you didn't break the third rule of hiking. I hope you brought water. I drank all of mine."

"I have water," said Molly. She searched in her rucksack for her leather water pouch. She'd packed it instead of her metal canteen because she felt the pouch was more like something Sacagawea would have carried. She pulled the pouch out now and discovered that it was empty. The water had leaked out all over everything in her rucksack.

Susan looked at the empty pouch and sighed.

Suddenly Molly felt ashamed. "Oh, Susan," she said. "I'm sorry. I was wrong about the downhill trail. Everyone else is probably already at the surprise. It's bad enough I got myself lost, but now I've got you lost, too. What are we going to do?"

"Well," said Susan with half a grin, "maybe you'd better smell the air again. Maybe that'll help us find the way."

Molly laughed in spite of herself. She took a deep, noisy breath. Susan giggled. Molly took another exaggerated breath. The odd thing was, Molly really *did* smell something.

"You know what?" she said. "I think I smell water. And I think I hear water, too. Come on."

Molly followed the rushing, gurgling sound through a clump of trees and down a little slope to a small stream.

"Hey!" said Susan. "The Sacagawea stuff worked!"

"Let's follow the stream," suggested Molly. "Maybe it leads to Lake Gowonagin."

"Okay," said Susan.

The two tired girls followed the stream as it twisted and turned its way through the woods. Then all of a sudden, the trees stopped. The stream had led them to a small clearing at the edge of a beautiful little pond. The pond water was dark, smooth, and peaceful.

"Ooh," breathed Susan and Molly together. Right away both girls sat down, kicked off their shoes, peeled off their socks, and dipped their feet in the cool water. *This is how Sacagawea must have felt when she finally put her feet in the Pacific Ocean*, Molly thought.

This is how Sacagawea must have felt when she finally put her feet in the Pacific Ocean, Molly thought.

195

Susan spoke in a soft voice. "I wonder if anyone has ever been here before."

"I don't know," said Molly. "Maybe we discovered it."

For a long while, Molly and Susan sat at the edge of the pond without saying a word, just resting and enjoying the feeling of sun on their faces. Then Susan sighed. "I hate to leave," she said. "But we'd better try to find our way back to camp."

Just then Molly heard the unmistakable sound of lots of feet stomping through the woods. "It's Miss Butternut and the girls!" she exclaimed joyfully. She jumped up and yelled, "Yoo-hoo! Over here! It's us!" This time, Molly was very happy to hear the hikers stampeding like a herd of elephants.

She was even more pleased to see them
as they appeared through the trees and
crowded around her and Susan. Everyone
was talking at once.

"Boy, did we have a time finding
you!" said Linda. "We thought you were
lost forever!"

"So did we!" said Susan.

"Girls!" said Miss Butternut in a voice
that made them immediately quiet. Her
round face was flushed. She put her
hands on her hips and said to Molly and
Susan, "Well. And what do you two have
to say for yourselves?"

Molly could hardly look Miss
Butternut in the eye. "It . . . it was all
my fault, Miss Butternut," she said,

shamefaced. "Susan just came after me to try to help me. I was the one who broke the rules of hiking. I won't do it again. I'm really sorry."

Miss Butternut shook her head. "The rules of hiking are not to be taken lightly," she said. "I think you've found *that* out."

Molly said, "I sure have."

Miss Butternut put one arm around Molly and the other around Susan. She looked out at the pond for a moment. Then she said, "And you've found something else, too. I've never seen this pond before. It's a beauty! What are you going to name it, girls?"

Molly and Susan looked at each other and smiled. "We'd like to call it

Sacagawea's Pond," said Molly. "Because she helped us find it."

"I am sure Sacagawea would be proud," said Miss Butternut. Then she said to the rest of the campers, "Who'd like a swim?"

"I would!" yelled the girls as they pulled their swimsuits out of their packs.

"Last one in is a rotten egg!" said Miss Butternut.

What a surprising day, thought Molly as she swam out to the middle of the pond. Suddenly she stopped still. The surprise! She had forgotten all about the surprise! "Linda!" she called out to her friend who was floating on her back nearby.

"What?" asked Linda lazily.

"Listen! When Susan and I were lost, did the rest of you find the surprise?"

"Yup," said Linda.

Molly couldn't stand it. "Well, come on! You've got to tell me. What is it? What's the surprise?" she demanded.

Without turning her head, Linda grinned. Right away Molly knew exactly what Linda was going to say, and she knew she deserved it. Sure enough, Linda answered, "I can't tell you what the surprise was. But, oh! You would have loved it!"

LOOKING BACK

THE STORY OF SACAGAWEA

At summer camp, Molly and her friends learned skills like those the pioneers used. Campers practiced starting a fire and building a shelter with only a blanket and sticks. When campers went on hikes, they learned how to identify birds and trees, read a compass, and follow trail markings. Miss Butternut and other counselors told stories about famous explorers like Lewis and Clark, who charted a trail through the wilderness 140 years before Molly's time.

Lewis and Clark's compass

*Lewis and Clark traveled from St. Louis, Missouri,
all the way to the Pacific Ocean.*

President Thomas Jefferson sent
Meriwether Lewis and William Clark to
explore the Louisiana Territory, the vast
lands bought by the United States in
1803. He wanted them to find a passage
over the Rocky Mountains to the Pacific
Ocean. In October 1804, Lewis and Clark
stopped to camp for the winter near a
Hidatsa Indian village in what is now

North Dakota. There they met a young woman named Sacagawea (sah-KAH-gah-we-ah).

Sacagawea was a Shoshone Indian who had been captured by the Hidatsas when she was about 12 years old. The Hidatsas gave her the name Sacagawea, or "Bird Woman." When she was 16, she was sold to a French-Canadian fur trader to be his wife.

When Lewis and Clark met Sacagawea, they hired her and her husband to join them on their journey. One reason Lewis and Clark hired them was to translate Indian languages. Sacagawea knew the Hidatsa and Shoshone languages, and her husband knew Hidatsa and French. When

Sacagawea meeting her husband at the Hidatsa Indian camp

the traveling group came upon Shoshone Indians, Sacagawea could translate into Hidatsa for her husband. Then he could translate into French, and someone in Lewis and Clark's group could translate into English—like a game of telephone!

In April 1805, the group set out on their journey. They had one addition—Sacagawea's new baby boy. His father named him Jean-Baptiste, but Clark nicknamed him "Pomp."

In May, Sacagawea helped the group avoid a disaster. The boat she was riding in hit a high wind and nearly capsized. Sacagawea rescued the tools, food and supplies, and medicine chest

A dugout canoe like the one Lewis and Clark used

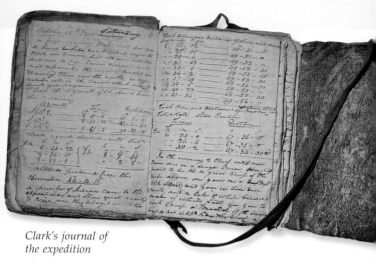

Clark's journal of the expedition

that almost floated away. If the group
had lost these items, they would have
had to turn back. Both Lewis and Clark
wrote in their journals that they were
impressed with Sacagawea's bravery and
calmness under pressure.

Lewis and Clark knew that to continue
their journey across the Rocky Mountains,

A painting of Shoshone horses

they would have to get horses from the Shoshones, Sacagawea's people. Lewis and Clark thought having a Shoshone in their group would help them get the horses they needed. For Sacagawea, this was a chance to see her people for the first time in many years.

In mid-August, the group found the Shoshones. Sacagawea cried with joy! Her brother was their chief. Lewis began

Lewis meeting the Shoshones

bargaining with the Shoshones for
the horses, but he found out that the
Shoshones were taking all of their horses
on a buffalo hunt. Sacagawea talked to
her brother and explained that the white
men had to have their horses before the
winter or their expedition would never

make it over the mountains. At last Sacagawea convinced him, and Lewis and Clark got the horses they needed to continue their journey.

That fall, Sacagawea kept the expedition safe when the group traveled through other Indian territories. Some of the Indians had never seen white men before, and they were prepared to defend their lands. But a war party never traveled with an Indian woman and a baby, so when the Indians saw Sacagawea and Pomp, they knew that the group came in peace.

Along the trail, Sacagawea helped the group gather roots and berries for food. She found prairie

Prairie turnip

210

turnips, wild artichokes, currants, and bitterroot. Lewis collected and pressed many of these plants so scientists could draw and name them.

Bitterroot

In November, the group was within 20 miles of its goal: the Pacific Ocean. A decision needed to be made—camp for the winter or press on to the ocean by foot. Everyone was given a vote in the decision, even Sacagawea. The group decided to set up camp.

By January 1806, Sacagawea had been near the ocean for more than a month and had still not seen it. One day, Clark was organizing a small group to find a whale that was beached on the ocean's shore.

The Pacific Ocean off the Oregon coast

The expedition was running out of food, and the whale meat could help them survive. Sacagawea asked to go along so she could see the great waters for herself. It was the chance of a lifetime.

The end of Sacagawea's story is a mystery. Some say she died in 1812, near where her journey started. Others say she returned to the Shoshones in Wyoming and lived to be nearly 100 years old.

What we do know about Sacagawea is that the country she helped explore did not forget her. Today there are at least three mountains, two lakes, and 23 monuments named for her. It is said that there are more monuments dedicated to Sacagawea than to any other woman in America.

A statue of Sacagawea and Jean-Baptiste in Bismarck, North Dakota

VALERIE TRIPP

At 9   Now

Valerie Tripp says that she became a
writer because of the kind of person
she is. She says she's curious, and writing
requires you to be interested in everything.
Talking is her favorite sport, and writing is a
way of talking on paper. She's a daydreamer,
which helps her come up with her ideas.
And she loves words. She even loves the
struggle to come up with just the right words
as she writes and rewrites. Ms. Tripp lives in
Maryland with her husband and daughter.

NICK BACKES

Nick Backes watched movies from the 1940s and looked at catalogues of clothes, furniture, and appliances to get to know Molly's world. Mr. Backes has two cats, Jack Benny and Lily, who keep him company by lying on his drawing table while he works at home in Oklahoma City.